Clumpety
BUMP

Essex County Council

'Clumpety Bump'
An original concept by Phil Allcock
© Phil Allcock

Illustrated by Richard Watson

Published by MAVERICK ARTS PUBLISHING LTD
Studio 3A, City Business Centre, 6 Brighton Road,
Horsham, West Sussex, RH13 5BB
© Maverick Arts Publishing Limited November 2018
+44 (0)1403 256941

A CIP catalogue record for this book is available at the British Library.

ISBN 978-1-84886-386-6

www.maverickbooks.co.uk

This book is rated as: Green Band (Guided Reading)
The original picture book text for this story has been
modified by the author to be an early reader.

Clumpety
BUMP

by **Phil Allcock**

illustrated by
Richard Watson

Clumpety Bump was a horse.
A lazy horse. A VERY lazy horse. He
didn't gallop. He didn't trot.
But he loved eating apples.

His owner, Wally Wobblebottom, liked to help people. He wished Clumpety would help him more.

But Clumpety was too lazy.

On Monday, Wally's friend Mrs Grumble was ill. So he set off on Clumpety Bump to take her some grapes.

Wally said, "Let's go across that field, Clumpety. Clippity clop, don't stop!"

But Clumpety Bump thought,
"I can't be bothered!"

He nibbled the chewy, gooey grass
instead. Wally jumped up and down
but he squashed the grapes.

SPLAT!

"Oh no!" he muttered.

On Tuesday, Wally took some chocolates to his friend, Jenny Penny.

Wally shouted, "Let's go across the stream, Clumpety. Slippity slop, don't stop!"

But Clumpety Bump thought,
"I can't be bothered!" So he drank
the dribbly, wibbly water instead.

SPLASH!

The chocolates floated away.

"Oh no!" cried Wally.

On Wednesday, they took some homemade jam to Wally's friend, Tom Toe.

Wally cried, "Let's go over that log, Clumpety. Zippity zop, don't stop!"

But Clumpety Bump thought, "I can't be bothered!" He stopped to nibble some yummy, scrummy leaves.

OUCH! Wally fell in some nettles
and the jam went everywhere.
"Oh no!" he yelled.

"I've had enough, Clumpety!"
Wally shouted.

"If you don't want to trot, gallop
or jump, you can stay at home!"

On Thursday, Wally wanted
to take flowers to his friend,
Ann Key. But he decided not
to take Clumpety...

19

He set off on his tractor instead.

BRRMMM
BRRMMM

But it got stuck in a big muddy puddle.

SQUELCH
SLURP

20

SPLOSH!

Wally tried to push it out, but
he slipped. "Oh no!"he groaned,
"I should have brought Clumpety!"

He went home to find Clumpety.

"I'm sorry I left you behind, Clumpety,"
said Wally, "but please can you help me?"

Clumpety grinned.

He wanted Wally to be happy again.

So off they went. Clumpety galloped across the field and didn't stop to eat the chewy, gooey grass.

He splashed across the stream and didn't stop to drink the dribbly, wibbly water.

He jumped over the log and didn't stop to nibble the yummy, scrummy leaves.

They soon reached Ann's house.

"Hello Ann," smiled Wally,

"I've brought you some..."

25

MUNCH!

"Oh no! Clumpety's eaten them!"

"Never mind!" grinned Ann, kissing him on the cheek. "Do you want to fetch an apple for Clumpety?"

"I can't be bothered!" replied Wally. "Oh no!" thought Clumpety.

"Only joking!" grinned Wally.

And he gave Clumpety the crunchiest,

munchiest apple ever.

Clumpety Bump was a horse.

A lively horse. A VERY lively horse.

He liked trotting, jumping and galloping.

And helping Wally.

And most of all, he loved eating apples.

Quiz

1. Clumpety Bump was a _____.
a) Dog
b) Horse
c) Boy

2. What does Wally want to take to Mrs Grumble?
a) Grapes
b) Flowers
c) Apples

3. Who is Wally taking the chocolates to?
a) Clumpety Bump
b) Mr Grumble
c) Jenny Penny

4. Why does Wally leave Clumpety at home?
a) Because he is too fast
b) Because he wants to help
c) Because he is too lazy

5. What does Clumpety get in the end?
a) The crunchiest, munchiest apple
b) Some jam
c) A tractor

Turn over for answers

Book Bands for Guided Reading

The colours on the left side represent the book banding scale:

Pink, Red, Yellow, Blue, Green, Orange, Turquoise, Purple, Gold, White

The Institute of Education book banding system is a scale of colours that reflects the various levels of reading difficulty. The bands are assigned by taking into account the content, the language style, the layout and phonics. Word, phrase and sentence level work is also taken into consideration.

Maverick Early Readers are a bright, attractive range of books covering the pink to white bands. All of these books have been book banded for guided reading to the industry standard and edited by a leading educational consultant.

To view the whole Maverick Readers scheme, visit our website at
www.maverickearlyreaders.com

Or scan the QR code above to view our scheme instantly!

Quiz Answers: 1b, 2a, 3c, 4c, 5a